The Winner's Wreath

Stories linking with the History
National Curriculum Key Stage 2

First published in 1999 by Franklin Watts
96 Leonard Street, London EC2A 4XD

Editor: Claire Berridge
Designer: Jason Anscomb
Consultant: Dr Anne Millard, BA Hons, Dip Ed, PhD

A CIP catalogue record for this book is available from the British Library.

ISBN 0 7496 3368 9 (hbk)
0 7496 3555 X (pbk)

Dewey Classification 938

Printed in Great Britain

The Winner's Wreath

by
Martin Oliver

Illustrations by Martin Remphry

1

Waiting

"Owww." Simonides groaned quietly. Something hard was digging into his left leg. He slowly rolled over, trying to get himself comfortable on the rocky ground. Through heavy eyes he saw the light of a dawn sky above. Befuddled by sleep,

Simonides managed to sit up. Where was he? What was he doing sleeping under the stars, wrapped in a thick blanket?

He turned over to where his father, Theron, was asleep beside him. Somewhere in the distance, Simonides heard a cough, a distant mutter and a quiet rustle. All around them, shadowy figures were lying on the ground or slowly waking up. Tents and the odd wooden hut dotted the hillside. As Simonides blinked

the sleep from his eyes, he spotted some early risers who were already washing themselves in the cold mountain water of the nearby river. In the distance, Simonides caught a glimpse of statues and a collection of imposing stone buildings amongst the trees. Suddenly he remembered why they were here – for the Olympic Games.

“Did you sleep well, son?”

Simonides turned round to see his

father stretching out and rubbing his back. "Now I know why no one else chose this spot. I think I'm getting too old for this camping out. Still, it'll all be worth it when we see Glaucus."

At the mention of his brother, a thrill of anticipation shivered down Simonides' neck. Glaucus was his big brother, four years older and due to compete in the boxing competition for boys. He had left over a month ago to join the other competitors and to practise his skills at the sacred site of Olympia.

"He'll be in action soon enough," Theron added. He smiled confidently at Simonides. "I'm sure he'll do us proud, eh?"

Despite his father's confidence, Simonides could hear a slight note of worry in Theron's voice. He glanced down at the mottled brown birthmark on the back of his left hand. The birthmark was small and unremarkable, but if it started to itch, it was a sign that trouble lay ahead. However, this morning it was fine, so Simonides nodded

in agreement and began to get dressed.

In a few well-practised movements, Simonides put on his tunic and tied his leather belt around his waist. The summer sun had already risen and was beginning to warm the air. Simonides decided not to wear his thicker chlamys (cloak) and he pulled on a pair of leather sandals instead of the boots that he usually kept for walking through the rugged countryside.

Simonides thought back to the long and dusty trek from their home in Euvovia. The journey had taken longer than they had expected and the sacred route had been thronged with other visitors and tradesmen. Unlike some of the more

prosperous spectators, they had walked all the way. By the time Simonides and his father had arrived last night, it hadn't been light enough to explore Olympia, so they had just found a place for the night.

Despite his excitement, Simonides had been worn out by the journey and soon fell asleep. Now, however, he was wide-awake and couldn't wait to see Glaucus and the games themselves.

"Not so fast," Theron laughed. "It's going to be a long day and we won't set off until we've got food in our bellies."

Simonides watched as his father broke

large pieces of bread from the loaf that they had bought the day before. He put it down on the ground before unwrapping some dried figs and olives that Simonides' mother had given them.

"To keep our strength up," he smiled, producing some cheese. "Now, let's eat ... and let's hope that Nike will look favourably upon Glaucus."

Simonides repeated the toast to the goddess of victory. Then he dipped the bread into the wine that had been diluted with water by Theron. Using his fingers, he scooped some of the cheese into his mouth. There was silence for a few minutes as father and son concentrated on finishing the food in front of them.

After a while, Theron belched loudly

and brushed some crumbs from his beard. "Now we can go. Let's visit Olympia."

2

The ploughshare

Simonides rushed down the Hill of Kronos, eager to explore. "Stay nearby," came Theron's warning. "It's going to be very busy down there."

Simonides slowed down so that he could walk beside his father. Theron was tall and broad-shouldered. His loosely tied himation revealed muscular arms and a thick, strong neck. Glaucus had inherited a similar physique, and the time he had spent working in the fields, had served to build up his strength. It was this strength that had led him to the Olympic Games – that, and a particular stone.

Simonides and Glaucus had been ploughing the ground with their father. It was hot, hard work, that was made more difficult by the stony ground they were trying to cultivate. Then bad luck had struck when the plough hit a stone. The impact had dislodged the ploughshare and Theron couldn't hammer it back into position. The field was a long way from their home and it looked like they would lose precious time, until Glaucus suggested that he could help. Using his bare fists, Glaucus punched the metal, battering it back into position. Theron and Simonides

were amazed at the power and accuracy of Glaucus' blows. Simonides had kept the stone, which was an unusual white colour and had a jagged edge, to remind him of his brother's strength.

It was a few weeks later that Theron had taken Glaucus to the gymnasium in the nearest town. They had come back in high spirits because they had met a trainer who had not only promised to give Glaucus basic boxing training, but had also suggested that they enter him for the Games, once he had fought in some local competitions.

That was how Glaucus had been sent off to the Games, and how Simonides and Theron found themselves joining the crowds who were heading for the Altis, the sacred olive grove at the heart of Olympia.

"It's changed quite a bit since I came here with my father," Theron told

Simonides as they followed the flow of people. "I can't remember there being so many of these treasuries before, but I do remember the important buildings. To the right – can you see that long square building? – that's the palaistra. Inside it is a courtyard, and that is where Glaucus has been training. The running events all take place on the flat piece of land to the left, and just behind that is the Hippodrome where the horses race."

Simonides could hardly take it all in. On their journey, his father had warned him how popular the Games were, but the scene before him was amazing. His eyes kept flicking from one sight to another. He had never seen so many grand buildings – nor had he seen so many people. Of course, he had been to market day with his brother, but even that was nothing compared to the crowds of people in front of him. It seemed as though the whole world was there.

As they got closer, the expectant buzz became recognisable as many hundreds of different voices. Everyone was talking Greek but in accents that Simonides had never heard before. He had never seen so many different groups of people before. To his right, proud tall Athenians were casting suspicious glances at their age-old rivals, the Spartans. A group of Corinthians strode purposefully past a gathering of men from Thrace. A troupe of acrobats

and jugglers were attracting a large crowd, while hawkers were selling their goods to the visitors. All around there was a hubbub and an air of excitement as people shouted, discussed and greeted each other in loud voices.

Simonides suddenly wanted to see Glaucus but before he could ask Theron where he might be, trumpets blared

deafeningly. Everyone fell silent and an expectant hush fell over the crowd.

"What's going on?" Simonides whispered.

"Just wait for a moment. You'll find out soon," said Theron.

The crowd jostled and moved forwards to get a better look. Simonides felt his father pick him up and put him on his shoulders. A pathway had been cleared among the spectators and Simonides heard a dull sound – the sound of many pairs of feet marching on stone slabs. Just then, the trumpets blared again. A line of trumpet players came into view, followed by another ...

and another. As the trumpeters continued with their journey around the Altis, Simonides glimpsed a swirl of colour. He made out a small group of men, clad in bright purple cloaks striding past, their heads held high.

"Who are they?" Simonides shouted above the din.

"They're the Olympic judges," Theron answered.

Simonides focused more clearly on the

group. He wondered what it must be like to be a judge. It was such a responsible job. Their route took them close to Simonides and he got a close look at one of the judges. He was a few years older than his father, slim with a neatly-kept beard, dark eyes and a stern expression. As the judge walked past, Simonides' father shouted up to him.

"Stop wriggling and scratching or you'll fall off."

Simonides realised that he had been scratching his birthmark, but the itching sensation vanished as the judges continued past him. Just then, wild applause broke out as another group appeared – the competitors. The noise from the crowd became even louder and Simonides was almost toppled over by the rush of spectators trying to get closer to their heroes.

Most people in the crowd had a favourite champion or were keen to show their support for the competitors from their

own city. Shouts of encouragement were echoed by other supporters or shouted down by their rivals. Simonides felt his stomach lurch with nerves – somewhere amongst them would be Glaucus.

As they came closer, Simonides saw how different the competitors were. At the front were the graceful, long-limbed runners. They seemed to bounce along on the balls of their feet, full of bottled-up

energy. Behind them came the heptathletes, their muscles tensed and ready for the trials ahead. But the loudest cheers of all came for the competitors in the physical sports – the wrestling, boxing

and the pankration.

"Come on, Arcesilas," shouted one section of the crowd while another was hushed by the sight of the mighty

Nicophon. Shorter and stockier than the other athletes, the neck muscles of these men bulged and they flexed their biceps trying to impress the crowd and intimidate their opponents.

At that moment, Theron whooped so loudly that Simonides almost fell off his shoulders. He immediately realised why. There, striding purposefully beside a small group of younger athletes was Glaucus. His dark hair was cut close to his skull and his muscles were clenched. Simonides waved and shouted and yelled his name but Glaucus strode on without seeing him.

"The training has done him good," Theron said. "He's looking stronger than I've ever seen him."

Simonides nodded but he couldn't help feeling a bit concerned when he saw some of the other competitors. Still, there was no time to worry, as his father started complaining that he was making his neck ache and lowered Simonides to the ground.

3

The glory of Zeus

The judges and competitors gathered in front of the most imposing building in Olympia. Twelve massive gleaming pillars supported the roof and steep white steps led up to the entrance. The temple itself was huge, dwarfing the crowds who

swarmed around it.

This was not the time to be polite. Pushing with all his strength, Theron led Simonides through the crowd. "Look inside," Theron instructed. "You will have never seen anything as wonderful."

Simonides gasped. In a day of amazing sights, this was the most incredible. Of course, he had heard tales of the gold and ivory statue of Zeus at Olympia but to actually see it took his breath away. It was the biggest statue he had ever seen. Zeus was sitting on a throne, staring out at the crowds. He was wearing an olive leaf crown and in his hand was a statue of the goddess of victory, Nike. Truly, thought Simonides, he is the King of the Gods.

The sun glinted off the golden crown of olive leaves, blinding Simonides. At that moment, the spectators surged forward. Sweat glistened on his brow and he suddenly became aware of just how little room he had to breathe. He felt his legs begin to buckle before his father was able to reach out a strong arm and clear a path through the crowds. Simonides allowed himself to be led away into the welcome shade of an olive tree, where Theron splashed water over his face.

"I ... I'm sorry father," Simonides spluttered. "It must have been the sun and the statue."

"Don't worry," came the reply. "Zeus has the same effect on many spectators. Just sit still and you'll soon be feeling better."

Despite his father's understanding words, Simonides didn't feel better. He had made them miss the judges' swearing-in ceremony and the opening day sacrifices.

"Do not trouble yourself," said Theron. "That is as nothing to the great procession and the ceremony that takes place on the third day of the Games. Three hundred oxen will be sacrificed to the glory of Zeus on the steps of his temple. If we are still here, we will be celebrating with our very own Olympic champion."

Could Glaucus really become an Olympic champion and wear the winner's wreath of olive leaves? Simonides' head

span at the idea. Just think of the honour it would bestow on the family and their town – not to mention the riches it would bring. For the last few months, he had hardly dared think about what a victory would mean, but now they were actually in Olympia and he had seen so many wonders, perhaps they would be lucky enough to see another. Or maybe luck had nothing to do with it. Perhaps the sacrifice that they had made before leaving would work. It had been made to Apollo, the god of boxing. If he had been pleased by their offerings, he might be watching over the contest and would maybe look kindly on Glaucus.

Perhaps it was because he was so busy daydreaming, or maybe because his brain was full of the things he had already seen, or it might just have been that he was so impatient to see his brother again – whatever the reason, the next few hours passed in a blur. Simonides hardly noticed the boys' race, he couldn't remember being led into the palaistra and he only had the vaguest memories of watching the wrestling competition. It was only when his father nudged him painfully in the ribs and he spotted a familiar figure amongst a small group of athletes, that he realised what was happening – the boxing was about to begin.

4

The fight

With his head held high, Glaucus stared at the crowd of spectators. His face was a mask, betraying no fear or sign of nerves. Like the other boxers, his skin glistened as the oil that coated his body shone in the sunlight. Simonides' attention was drawn to

something that he had never seen before – the strips of stout leather that were tightly bound around the knuckles on both of his brother's hands and extended up around his forearms.

"Just wait until Glaucus' opponents feel the sting from his 'ants'," Theron shouted excitedly.

Simonides nodded and tried to ignore the unpleasant knotted feeling in his stomach. Although his brother certainly looked formidable, so did his opponents. One particularly tough-looking character worried Simonides. He was huge, with massive arm muscles and he was encouraging the crowd to cheer him.

"I hope Glaucus doesn't have to fight him," Simonides thought. Cauliflower ears and a broken nose were witnesses to hard-fought contests in the past. "How old is he?"

"If he's under 18, he qualifies."

"But how can you tell? He looks older than that."

"That's up to the judges to decide. If he's here, he must have proved his age."

At the mention of the judges, Simonides spotted a familiar-looking man in a purple robe. At that moment, his hand began to itch and Simonides started to scratch his birthmark. This was not a good omen, but Simonides breathed a sigh of relief when he saw that lots had already been drawn and that his brother would not be fighting the giant. He put all thoughts of him and the judge out of his mind as the other boxers left the fighting area, leaving Glaucus and his first opponent alone.

The contest began with a flurry of fists. Simonides winced as he saw the damage that the punches were inflicting, but his brother was brave and strong. He took what was thrown at him and returned it with interest. His first opponent was soon knocked out, and another eventually retired as Glaucus fought his way into the final.

Just one more boxer lay in the way of Glaucus being crowned Olympic champion – but what an obstacle. As Simonides had feared, Glaucus was up against the giant who had quickly disposed of his opponents and was looking increasingly confident. By contrast, Simonides could see that Glaucus' fights had taken a great toll of his strength. His lack of experience meant that he had suffered badly. His right eye was swollen, his lips were puffy and blood had dried from a dozen cuts around his face.

The fight began and the giant immediately launched his attack, eager to finish the contest. The crowd

whooped and roared as Glaucus reeled back, raising his arms in a desperate effort to ward off the punches.

"Don't try and fight him," yelled Simonides. "Stay out of his reach."

Whether his brother heard or whether he had the same survival instinct, Glaucus did exactly what Simonides hoped. Instead of trading blows, he tried to keep out the way of his opponent's huge punches. He danced and ducked below the flailing fists, then darted in to land some hits of his own.

For a while, Glaucus' tactics worked. Simonides shouted his support until his voice was hoarse. The giant roared in frustration and anger as carefully placed blows missed their target but then, more by luck than judgement, one of his punches

landed, knocking Glaucus off balance and doubling him up in pain. The crowd cheered – except for Simonides and Theron. Glaucus was only a few yards from them and Simonides could see the dazed look on his brother's face.

The giant lowered his guard and began winding up for the final bone-crunching blow.

"Surely the judge will stop the fight," shouted Theron. "Otherwise ..."

As his father's voice trailed off, Simonides looked at the angry scratches on the back of his left hand. One thing was for sure, Glaucus was on his own. The judge wasn't going to spare him. Simonides couldn't bear to see what was about to

happen. He looked down at the ground and his gaze was caught by a large stone. The stone was white and had a jagged edge – just like the one that had damaged the ploughshare all those months ago.

In a flash, a thought came to Simonides. He looked up as the giant advanced towards Glaucus who was staring blindly in his direction. A hush settled on the crowd as they waited for the killer punch and in that split second of

silence, Simonides shouted, "remember the ploughshare."

A spark of recognition lit up in Glaucus' eyes and Simonides watched him shake his head, trying to clear his

thoughts. He turned round just in time to duck under the giant's punch and to deliver his own reply. There was a cracking sound and a look of puzzlement spread over his opponent's face, shortly before he sank to his knees and fell face first into the dust.

Simonides and Theron were the first to reach Glaucus. Simonides grabbed a wet cloth and squeezed it over his brother's face. "You did it," he whispered. "You really did it."

But how was Glaucus? He had suffered such a pounding, what sort of state was he in? Before Simonides could check his condition, the crowd began shouting the name of the new champion and lifted the trio onto their shoulders.

From his vantage point, Simonides saw the look of disappointment on the judge's face as Glaucus was carried before him. Faced with the cheering spectators, the judge had no choice but to crown him with the winner's wreath of olive leaves.

"Thanks be to Apollo, thanks be to Zeus," Theron shouted. "What do you say, Glaucus? Tonight we shall have a feast to celebrate your victory and thank the gods."

Glaucus said nothing and a flicker of worry crossed Simonides' brow. Then his brother gazed back at him. His battered and bruised face broke into a smile before he croaked, "and thanks be to Simonides – and the ploughshare."

Notes

The Background

According to Greek legends, the first Olympic Games were held in 776BC. These stories tell how the Games were founded by Heracles (who the Romans called Hercules) to celebrate the completion of one of his twelve tasks.

The Games were held every four years in Olympia and they continued for almost 1,000 years. Before each new Games were due to begin, heralds travelled far and wide to spread the news and to announce that a three month truce from fighting would be held. Even the bitterest enemies would stop fighting so that the contestants and the spectators could reach Olympia safely.

Zeus – King of the Gods

The Games always took place in summer and lasted for five days, but not all of this time was taken up with sport. The Games were dedicated to Zeus and prayers and sacrifices were offered to all the Gods. Olympia became one of the holiest places in Ancient Greece, with huge temples and statues dedicated to the gods.

The Events

Over the 1,000 years of the Olympic Games, many different sports were tried, and some like mule–racing were quickly dropped. The Greeks invented the Pentathlon which included running, long-jumping, discuss, javelin and wrestling. Athletes also competed in sprint races and in one event the contestants wore armour.

Chariot and horse races were popular with rich members of Greek society. Although some of them didn't drive themselves, they provided the horses and equipment for the races and were crowned as Olympic champions if they won.

The Ancient Greeks were often at war with each other, so it's no surprise that some of the most popular events were the combat sports – boxing, wrestling and the pankration (a mixture of both boxing and wrestling). These sports were open to both adults and to athletes under 18.

The Judges

Olympic judges always wore purple robes and came from Elis, a small town near Olympia. Judges swore to be honest and fair. However, in the boys events when the rules stated that athletes had to be under 18, it would have been very hard to prove a competitor's age as nobody carried written documents.

If judges or competitors were found cheating, they could be fined or even whipped. The money raised from fines was put towards building a statue of Zeus.

Spot the difference

There were many differences between the Greek Olympic Games and the ones we know today.

1. Free admission. There was no charge for spectators although there wasn't much in the way of facilities. About 40,000 spectators could watch the games. The judges and a few rich spectators had seats but most people had to watch from the surrounding hillsides.
2. Only one winner was recognised. Second and third places did not count.

The winner received an olive wreath cut from a sacred tree in Olympia.

3. Most athletes competed without clothes.

4. No women were allowed to compete in the Games and it is thought that they weren't even allowed to watch. If a woman was discovered, her punishment was to be thrown off a high cliff.

Sparks: Historical Adventures

ANCIENT GREECE

The Great Horse of Troy – The Trojan War
0 7496 3369 7 (hbk) 0 7496 3538 X (pbk)
The Winner's Wreath – Ancient Greek Olympics
0 7496 3368 9 (hbk) 0 7496 3555 X (pbk)

INVADERS AND SETTLERS

Boudicca Strikes Back – The Romans in Britain
0 7496 3366 2 (hbk) 0 7496 3546 0 (pbk)
Viking Raiders – A Norse Attack
0 7496 3089 2 (hbk) 0 7496 3457 X (pbk)
Erik's New Home – A Viking Town
0 7496 3367 0 (hbk) 0 7496 3552 5 (pbk)

TALES OF THE ROWDY ROMANS

The Great Necklace Hunt
0 7496 2221 0 (hbk) 0 7496 2628 3 (pbk)
The Lost Legionary
0 7496 2222 9 (hbk) 0 7496 2629 1 (pbk)
The Guard Dog Geese
0 7496 2331 4 (hbk) 0 7496 2630 5 (pbk)
A Runaway Donkey
0 7496 2332 2 (hbk) 0 7496 2631 3 (pbk)

TUDORS AND STUARTS

Captain Drake's Orders – The Armada
0 7496 2556 2 (hbk) 0 7496 3121 X (pbk)
London's Burning – The Great Fire of London
0 7496 2557 0 (hbk) 0 7496 3122 8 (pbk)
Mystery at the Globe – Shakespeare's Theatre
0 7496 3096 5 (hbk) 0 7496 3449 9 (pbk)
Plague! – A Tudor Epidemic
0 7496 3365 4 (hbk) 0 7496 3556 8 (pbk)
Stranger in the Glen – Rob Roy
0 7496 2586 4 (hbk) 0 7496 3123 6 (pbk)
A Dream of Danger – The Massacre of Glencoe
0 7496 2587 2 (hbk) 0 7496 3124 4 (pbk)
A Queen's Promise – Mary Queen of Scots
0 7496 2589 9 (hbk) 0 7496 3125 2 (pbk)
Over the Sea to Skye – Bonnie Prince Charlie
0 7496 2588 0 (hbk) 0 7496 3126 0 (pbk)

TALES OF A TUDOR TEARAWAY

A Pig Called Henry
0 7496 2204 4 (hbk) 0 7496 2625 9 (pbk)
A Horse Called Deathblow
0 7496 2205 9 (hbk) 0 7496 2624 0 (pbk)
Dancing for Captain Drake
0 7496 2234 2 (hbk) 0 7496 2626 7 (pbk)
Birthdays are a Serious Business
0 7496 2235 0 (hbk) 0 7496 2627 5 (pbk)

VICTORIAN ERA

The Runaway Slave – The British Slave Trade
0 7496 3093 0 (hbk) 0 7496 3456 1 (pbk)
The Sewer Sleuth – Victorian Cholera
0 7496 2590 2 (hbk) 0 7496 3128 7 (pbk)
Convict! – Criminals Sent to Australia
0 7496 2591 0 (hbk) 0 7496 3129 5 (pbk)
An Indian Adventure – Victorian India
0 7496 3090 6 (hbk) 0 7496 3451 0 (pbk)
Farewell to Ireland – Emigration to America
0 7496 3094 9 (hbk) 0 7496 3448 0 (pbk)
The Great Hunger – Famine in Ireland
0 7496 3095 7 (hbk) 0 7496 3447 2 (pbk)
Fire Down the Pit – A Welsh Mining Disaster
0 7496 3091 4 (hbk) 0 7496 3450 2 (pbk)
Tunnel Rescue – The Great Western Railway
0 7496 3353 0 (hbk) 0 7496 3537 1 (pbk)
Kidnap on the Canal – Victorian Waterways
0 7496 3352 2 (hbk) 0 7496 3540 1 (pbk)
Dr. Barnardo's Boys – Victorian Charity
0 7496 3358 1 (hbk) 0 7496 3541 X (pbk)
The Iron Ship – Brunel's Great Britain
0 7496 3355 7 (hbk) 0 7496 3543 6 (pbk)
Bodies for Sale – Victorian Tomb-Robbers
0 7496 3364 6 (hbk) 0 7496 3539 8 (pbk)
Penny Post Boy – The Victorian Postal Service
0 7496 3362 X (hbk) 0 7496 3544 4 (pbk)
The Canal Diggers – The Manchester Ship Canal
0 7496 3356 5 (hbk) 0 7496 3545 2 (pbk)
The Tay Bridge Tragedy – A Victorian Disaster
0 7496 3354 9 (hbk) 0 7496 3547 9 (pbk)
Stop, Thief! – The Victorian Police
0 7496 3359 X (hbk) 0 7496 3548 7 (pbk)
A School – for Girls! – Victorian Schools
0 7496 3360 3 (hbk) 0 7496 3549 5 (pbk)
Chimney Charlie – Victorian Chimney Sweeps
0 7496 3351 4 (hbk) 0 7496 3551 7 (pbk)
Down the Drain – Victorian Sewers
0 7496 3357 3 (hbk) 0 7496 3550 9 (pbk)
The Ideal Home – A Victorian New Town
0 7496 3361 1 (hbk) 0 7496 3553 3 (pbk)
Stage Struck – Victorian Music Hall
0 7496 3363 8 (hbk) 0 7496 3554 1 (pbk)

TRAVELS OF A YOUNG VICTORIAN

The Golden Key
0 7496 2360 8 (hbk) 0 7496 2632 1 (pbk)
Poppy's Big Push
0 7496 2361 6 (hbk) 0 7496 2633 X (pbk)
Poppy's Secret
0 7496 2374 8 (hbk) 0 7496 2634 8 (pbk)
The Lost Treasure
0 7496 2375 6 (hbk) 0 7496 2635 6 (pbk)

20th-CENTURY HISTORY

Fight for the Vote – The Suffragettes
0 7496 3092 2 (hbk) 0 7496 3452 9 (pbk)
The Road to London – The Jarrow March
0 7496 2609 7 (hbk) 0 7496 3132 5 (pbk)
The Sandbag Secret – The Blitz
0 7496 2608 9 (hbk) 0 7496 3133 3 (pbk)
Sid's War – Evacuation
0 7496 3209 7 (hbk) 0 7496 3445 6 (pbk)
D-Day! – Wartime Adventure
0 7496 3208 9 (hbk) 0 7496 3446 4 (pbk)
The Prisoner – A Prisoner of War
0 7496 3212 7 (hbk) 0 7496 3455 3 (pbk)
Escape from Germany – Wartime Refugees
0 7496 3211 9 (hbk) 0 7496 3454 5 (pbk)
Flying Bombs – Wartime Bomb Disposal
0 7496 3210 0 (hbk) 0 7496 3453 7 (pbk)
12,000 Miles From Home – Sent to Australia
0 7496 3370 0 (hbk) 0 7496 3542 8 (pbk)